An Evening at Alfie's

For Dorothy Edwards

A Red Fox Book
Published by Random House Children's Books
20 Vauxhall Bridge Road, London SW1V 2SA
A division of Random House UK Ltd
London Melbourne Sydney Auckland
Johannesburg and agencies throughout the world
Copyright © Shirley Hughes 1984
1 3 5 7 9 10 8 6 4 2
First published by The Bodley Head Children's Books 1984
Red Fox edition 1995
Printed in Hong Kong
RANDOM HOUSE UK Limited Reg. No. 954009
ISBN 0 09 992710 1

An Evening at Alfie's

Shirley Hughes

Red Fox

One cold, winter evening . . .

Alfie and his little sister, Annie Rose, were
all ready for bed,

Mum and Dad were all ready to go out,

and Mrs MacNally's Maureen was in the living-room.
She had come to look after Alfie and Annie Rose
while Mum and Dad went to a party.

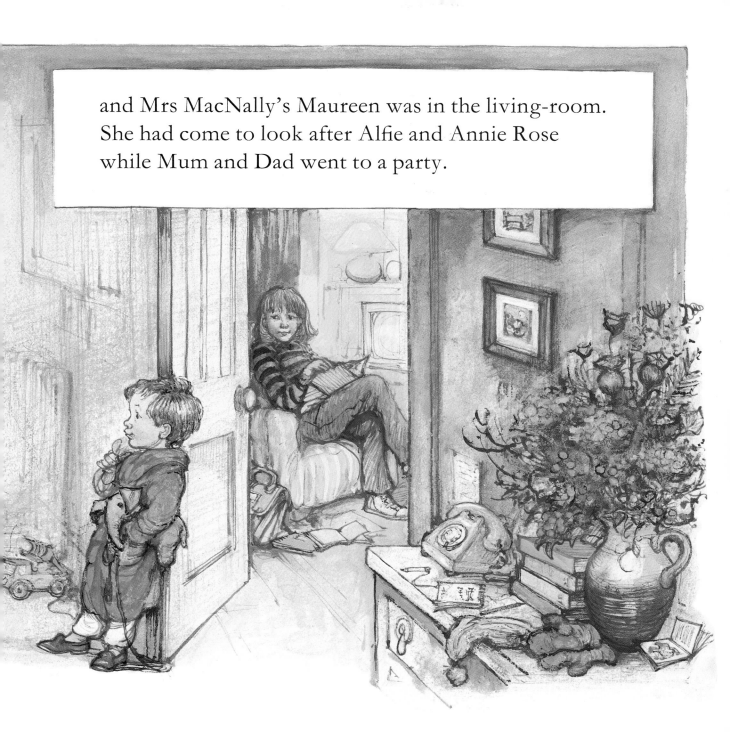

Alfie and Maureen waved good-bye to them from the window.

Annie Rose was already in her cot. Soon she settled down and went to sleep.

Alfie liked Maureen. She always read him a
story when she came to baby-sit.

Tonight Alfie wanted the story about Noah
and his Ark full of animals. Alfie liked to hear
how the rain came drip, drip, drip, and then
splash! splash! splash! and then rushing
everywhere, until the whole world was
covered with water.

When Maureen had finished the story it was time for Alfie to go to bed. She came upstairs to tuck him up. They had to be very quiet and talk in whispers in case they woke up Annie Rose.

Maureen gave Alfie a good-night hug and went off downstairs, leaving the door a little bit open.

Alfie didn't feel sleepy. He lay in bed
looking at the patch of light on the ceiling. For
a long time all was quiet. Then he heard a
funny noise outside on the landing.

Alfie sat up. The noise was just outside his door. Drip, drip, drip! Soon it got quicker. It changed to drip-drip, drip-drip, drip-drip! It was getting louder too.

Alfie got out of bed and peeped round the door. There was a puddle on the floor. He looked up. Water was splashing into the puddle from the ceiling, drip-drip, drip-drip, drip-drip! It was raining inside the house!

Alfie went downstairs. Maureen was doing
her homework in front of the television.
"It's raining on the landing," Alfie told her.

Alfie and Maureen went back upstairs. The puddle was getting bigger. The drip-drip, drip-drip, drip-drip had turned into a splash! splash! splash!

"Hmm, looks like a burst pipe," said Maureen. A plumber was one of the things she wanted to be when she left school.

"Better get a bucket," she said. So Alfie showed her where the bucket was kept, in the kitchen cupboard with the brushes and brooms.

But now the water was
dripping down in another
place. Alfie and Maureen
found two of Mum's big
mixing bowls and put them
underneath the drips.

Maureen got on the telephone to her Mum. The MacNallys lived just across the street. Mrs MacNally was there in a moment.

"Oh dear, oh dear, it's ruining your mother's floor!" cried Mrs MacNally. "Fetch some floor-cloths, Maureen!"

Just then Annie Rose woke up and began to cry.
"Shh, shh, there, there," said Mrs MacNally,
bending over her cot. But Annie Rose
only looked at her and cried louder.

Mrs MacNally ran back out to the landing. She and Maureen tried to mop up the water. But now the drips were coming from lots of different places, splash, splash, splash!

"We ought to turn the water off from the main," said Maureen, "but I don't know how you do it. I think I'd better fetch Dad."

While she was gone Mrs MacNally mopped
and mopped, and emptied brimming bowls,
and in between mopping and emptying she ran
to try to comfort Annie Rose. But Annie Rose
went on crying and crying. The drips on the
landing came faster and faster.

Now there were a lot of puddles on the floor. Alfie paddled in them for a while. It was quite fun but the water was very cold. He thought that soon perhaps the whole street would be covered with water and they would all have to float away in a boat, like Noah's Ark.

Soon Maureen came running upstairs with Mr MacNally close behind her, wearing his bedroom slippers.

"What's all this, then?" said Mr MacNally, looking at all the water pouring down.

He put his head round the
bedroom door. He and Annie
Rose were old friends.

"Dear, dear, what's all this?"
he said in a very kind voice.

Then he went downstairs
and found a large sort of tap
under the stairs and turned it
off, just like that.

"So *that's* where it was,"
said Maureen.

Then the water stopped pouring down
through the ceiling, splash! splash! splash! and
became a drip-drip, drip-drip, drip-drip,

and then a drip. . . drip. . . . drip. . . . . drip. . . . . .
and then it stopped altogether.

"Oh, thank goodness for
that!" said Mrs MacNally.

"I'll know how to do it
next time," said Maureen.

But Annie Rose was still crying.

Alfie went into the bedroom to
see if he could cheer her up. Tears
were rolling down her cheeks
and soaking into her blanket.

"Don't cry, Annie Rose," said Alfie. And he put his hand through the bars of her cot and patted her very gently, as he had seen Mum do sometimes.

Annie Rose still wore nappies at night.

"Annie Rose is wet," Alfie told everyone. "And her bed's wet too. I expect that's why she's crying."

"Why, so she is, poor little mite!" said Mrs MacNally.

When Annie Rose was all dry and comfortable again, Mrs MacNally put her on the living-room sofa with Alfie and tucked a quilt round them. Then she gave them both a biscuit.

Annie Rose was quite cheerful now. She got very friendly with Mr MacNally and he let her play a game with him, taking off his glasses and putting them on again. Then she sucked her thumb and leaned up against Alfie, and Alfie leaned up against her. When Mum and Dad came home, they were both fast asleep.

Next morning Mum told Alfie not to turn on the taps until the plumber had been to mend the burst pipe.

Alfie didn't mind not having a wash. He'd had enough water the evening before to last for a long time.